To Abby, Hannah & Sam,
Love Auntie Pat   ♡

To my mom, the best teacher of all of the fairies' lessons

Thank you!

♥

Claire

www.mascotbooks.com

# Santa's Fairy Helpers

**For more information, please contact:**
Mascot Books
620 Herndon Parkway #320
Herndon, VA 20170
info@mascotbooks.com

Library of Congress Control Number: 2019903983

CPSIA Code: PRT0519A
ISBN-13: 978-1-64543-050-6

Printed in the United States

# Santa's Fairy Helpers

## An enchanted
## Christmas countdown

Written by **Claire Saeli May**

Illustrated by Anastasia Khmelevska

Here is a story
that you may have never been told
about Santa's fairy helpers...

They are scattered throughout, in towns all around,
and report to dear Santa all the good they have found.

Their job is simple, so please remember,
they watch how you act every day in December.

The first week of December,
the **Red Fairies** sneak out
to hear the kind words
children whisper and shout.

"Come on over to play and join in the fun!"
Red Fairies smile when you include everyone.

The second week of December,
it's the **Green Fairies'** turn
to report to dear Santa
all that they learn.

They look for good deeds
children do through the day,
like picking up toys
after they play.

Week three of December,
you are given a test.
Can you use your manners
as a host and a guest?

Santa's **Silver Fairies** are sparkling among trees,

making sure children say "thank you" and "please."

The week before Christmas,
Santa's dearest friends will show
shimmering all golden,
their Christmas spirit aglow.

The job of the **Gold Fairies**
is the most important to do—
they find the Christmas spirit
shining in you!

Santa and his fairies have a
special message for you...

For if you try
to be the best you can be
Santa may surprise you
with something
under
the
tree!

# About the Author

**Claire Saeli May** grew up in a happy, love-filled home as the youngest of seven children. When she was a little girl, her mom would tell stories about Santa's Fairies and would often "see" them in the weeks before Christmas. Of course, this motivated Claire to be a very good girl!

Today, Claire is living her dream as a wife, mother, and teacher. Claire lives in Buffalo, New York, with her husband Joe and is proud of her three grown children, Eric, Brigit, and Alex, who spent many childhood days looking for the fairies.

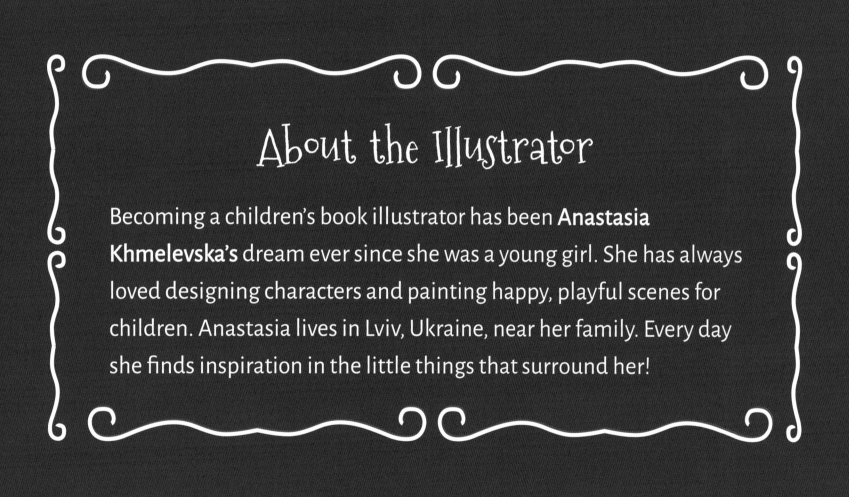

## About the Illustrator

Becoming a children's book illustrator has been **Anastasia Khmelevska's** dream ever since she was a young girl. She has always loved designing characters and painting happy, playful scenes for children. Anastasia lives in Lviv, Ukraine, near her family. Every day she finds inspiration in the little things that surround her!